UNAPOLOGETIC SCRIBBLES

A JOURNEY OF BROKEN EXPECTATIONS

MONICA

*"This book is dedicated to my one true love "Tzar"
who came into my life like an angel, gave me a
reason to be actually happy and live, and showered
me with his unconditional love.
In every manner, he made me a better person,
capable of loving, nourishing, and fearing
[obviously in a healthy way].*

*He is classified as a dog, but I have not seen more
humanity in any humans than in him. He cannot
read this but I am so proud to be a mother of this
baby.*

I Love You...Always and Forever."

Contents

PREFACE

I have seen many people around me suffering in bad marriages and toxic relationships for their entire life and choosing to stay in that. Sometimes due to their kids, sometimes due to society, sometimes due to their own financial instability, sometimes just being addicted to someone, sometimes due to the lack of courage, sometimes due to fear to change, sometimes due to their lifestyle, sometimes because they do not get any help, sometimes due to their morals and ethics, sometimes due to the time they have invested, sometimes they are not sure if it is really toxic, sometimes they are way too submissive, sometimes just because they cannot live alone, sometimes because there is an illusion of love, and sometimes we just came up with excuses of choosing to stay due to our own incompetencies. I have seen people fighting, abusing, crying, and still staying. This is not love. It never is. A person that loves you can never hurt you in any manner and if it is hurting, it's not meant to be.

I am always a firm believer in being strong and being self-sufficient. But seeing all these things around literally hurts me. I can't imagine a woman being so weak but it's the reality that a woman doesn't know what she is capable of.

I started working on this book 2 years ago but finding a correct story to depict this was difficult. I knew what to want to tell the world but binding my thought into a perfect story was something I was working on. I met a lot of people and tried to know their experiences, heard their stories, and a bit of something that I too experienced. This story is not just about a bad relationship involving marriage or romantic aspects but an overall relationship that could be within a family. How the things in a toxic environment can never grow into something beautiful. Things are hard but standing against those hard things is what makes you much alive and a life worth living.

Choosing a relationship is sometimes a choice and sometimes not but where to end it is always a choice. We come across hundreds of people in a single life and no one is perfect and it is fine but if the imperfection of others became a reason for your sleepless nights then it is worth giving a thought, try and find what you are fighting for, and is there any chance you deserve that.

Acknowledgements

I would like to thank Vaibhav for not only being a support in my journey as a writer but being a partner in my life.

Life always gives us two choices to stand by or leave. Obviously, giving up on anything is quite easy and relief but supporting and standing together with each other through the tough is difficult. Thank you for proving every time that you are a person I can count upon. Any person who had you in their life would be very lucky and I am honored to say that I am one of them. To be honest, I do not believe in God, but after being with you it feels like yes there is a power above everyone and I have all my faith in you.

We met many people in our lives but there are only a few ones that leave an imprint on your soul. Thank you for touching my soul, guiding me with things, and just blindly supporting all my dreams. Thank you for filling me with positivity and with you being right by my side, it feels like nothing bad can ever happen, and even if it does we have the power to overcome it together.

It is an amazing feeling how being with you makes me feel both strong and weak [in a good way] at the same time. Thank you for being such an amazing human being and I am nothing but proud to share this life with you.

ACKNOWLEDGMENTS

PROLOGUE

This story is not only about Bikram and Parvati, it covers before and beyond. Their kids, the society, and everything that contributed to their not-so-happy endings. These are characters but this story is dedicated to and inspired by the life of approximately 40 percent of families around the globe. Situations might differ from person to person but is a hard reality of the things not being discussed or simply ignored.

It's often said in India that marriages are for eternity. And there's even data to support it: According to the UN Women's Progress of the World's Women report, India has one of the lowest divorce rates in the world.

However, this does not necessarily mean these marriages are happy; in fact, according to the National Crime Records Bureau's (NCRB) data in recent years, a higher number of those in unhappy marriages seem to be choosing death over divorce. According to the NCRB report, on suicides in India, marital problems have driven about 37,591 people to suicide between 2016 and 2020 — an average of about 20 people daily. Out of these, divorce has driven 2,688 people (about 7 percent of the total) to end their lives. This means 13 times as many people died by suicide due to non-divorce-related issues.

The report also shows that the number of women who committed suicide owing to 'marriage-related issues' was more than that of men. Extramarital affairs caused 1,100 suicides per year or a five-year total of 5,737 and the biggest reason for suicide is depression, which is "poorly accounted for".

If a bad marriage is troubling you mentally, staying in it will pain you 24 hours a day. But if you separate yourself from that atmosphere, that toxicity, and reduce the suffering to either one hour a day or to none at all — you are emotionally well-off — which could explain the low suicide rate among divorcees.

Lastly, this story is not to hurt anyone's feelings or perceptions and all the characters depicted are strictly fictitious and any kind of resemblance to anyone known or unknown, dead or alive is purely coincidental The motive of this story is to create awareness about the unspoken topics through a nice story-telling.

I

Broken Dreams

Before, I begin, this is not just a story. It's a journey of a woman - her love, her sacrifice, and ultimately killing her soul. It's not just a story but a voice she never raised or the voice which was never listened to.

She was a dreamer, but her dreams were crushed, and the betrayal burnt her soul. I will not say it is just a story, this is a journey of 30 years of betrayal by everyone she knew, she trusted.

I believe this story goes back to the early 1980s and I am not even born yet. Even my parents have not started planning for me yet. Though this story started in the 80s, this journey will be full of twists and turns and will show you all of the 90s, and 2000s till today.

It's still the old Indian society, especially in rural India where the girl child was married away before she hit 17 years.

On the foothills of the Himalayas, there was a small yet beautiful village that is covered with snow in the winters and summers were also pleasant. In that village, there lived a little girl - beautiful, full of life, full of dreams, obedient and what's it's called in Indian society- sanskari, sarvagurn sampan Kanya.

She goes to a nearby village school every morning and comes home in the afternoon. After which she plays with her siblings and friends and helps her mother with the household work. This little girl was intelligent, smart, and wanted an education and be something in her life but sadly, it seems like fate had some other plans for her and as an obedient daughter, she never protested her family's decision. It was happening to everyone around her with the girls of the same age group but nevertheless, the marriage institution did not break her dream to learn and gain knowledge. This girl was a perfectionist on every task which was ever given to her and she was determined to embrace and excel in this new chapter of her life which was about to happen.

By some known relatives, a perfect match was chosen for this little girl named Parvati, and the boy and his family came to see the girl. She was asked to bring tea by her father and when Parvati arrived with the tray, it felt as if heaven had sent one of its goddesses.

Her eyes were down looking at the serving tray, her dupatta was over her head and after she poured tea for everyone, she went ahead and touched the feet of all the elders in the room for their blessings. His potential husband was sitting right there but she was too shy to raise her head in front of the elders even to get a glimpse of this young man. Her heart was beating fast as if she had missed a train. She went inside so quickly after serving tea as if she has seen a ghost.

Yeah, right. That was the marriage institution back in the 80s and definitely feels like the plot of an old Bollywood film.

After a while, when the guests were gone, Parvati's father came to the room where her mother, herself, and her sisters and brothers were sitting and told, "*they liked Parvati very much and would like to make her their daughter in law. I also liked that kid, he is educated, working in the city, and has a government job. Parvati would be lucky to be his wife and thus if you agree, I will go to their place next week to fix the date.*"

Obviously, this information was not for Parvati, and neither did she has a say in it. If she liked the boy or not or even if she is ready for marriage or not. But her mother seems happy and without any further questions asked she quickly said, "*if you like the family and think it is the right thing to do, then it is a yes from our side as well and we shall start the marriage preparations. Oh yes, spring seems to be auspicious time*".

The father as said, went to the boy's place the next week and presented a few gifts as a confirmation of the marriage proposal from their end, and with the blessings of all elders in both the families a perfect day was fixed.

Marriage preparations started and a few months later, with the blossoming of spring, the big day of Parvati's life came. She walked down the aisle in a maroon velvet lehenga with a golden handcrafted design in it. She was fair and looked nothing less than a goddess in that maroon dress. Her head was down as if she was counting the stone blocks on the floor and her face was covered with an orange and golden viel. Her heart was beating very fast as she took small steps towards the Mandap. She was happyily anxious and nervous as the marriage rituals proceeded.

Soon the *Pandit* asked to get up for *pheras.* As she was taking her circles around that fire [as a part of the Hindu marriage ritual], she took a look around from her veil and saw her parents, siblings, friends, neighbors, and house, and plenty of thoughts came into her mind - "*she had to leave her home where she was born, played with her siblings in the lawn, spent 17 years of her life knowing that it is a place she can count on, knowing where to come back after school, those parents with whom she knew she would be protected- but one day she needs to just leave all these things and go to a totally different family full of strangers. Why cannot live at her own home forever and with her own family?*" Thinking about all these things and an unforeseen future, all the memories came flooding her mind and tears started to roll down her pink cheeks. Parvati felt so anxious, weak, and unprotected that finally, she broke down into uncontrollable tears at the time of *Bidaai.* But the fun fact was she cannot even cry her heart out. She was a girl and whatever she was feeling, was taught to be normal. She needs to stop crying as it was time to go with her husband to her own house and start her own new journey in life.

Parvati began her new journey of approximately 5-6 hours from her parent's house to her husband's house wherein, for the first time she peeped out of the window through her veil and saw all those high mountains and small waterfall and she was amazed to see this beauty of nature. She was the time being forgot about her parents and old house but was just thrilled to see all these roads and cars and everything and suddenly the bus stopped. Her husband asked her to get down and they walked toward his home.

Now, she was not thrilled anymore but was nervous to meet her in-laws for the first time. As they are coming closer to the house, Parvati was now assuming what their in-laws be like, if they will like her, what will happen if she make any mistake - will they scold her or they will treat her like their own daughter. With all these weird thoughts running through her mind, they reached the front lawn of the house where all the family members, relatives, and neighbors were gathered. She was welcomed to her new house by her new family and it was the first night after her wedding.

By the time they reached the house, it was already late evening so after having dinner with all the family members, Parvati was escorted to her husband's bedroom. The room was big with a bed in the middle and two pillows. There was a white bedsheet on the bed and the bed was beautifully decorated with rose petals and the light of the room was a bit dim. She went ahead and sat on the corner of the bed. Parvati was very tired due to the long journey but her heart was racing a thousand miles per second. She was alone in that big, dark room and was nervous but was waiting for her husband whom she never talked to or even seen properly before marriage.

Many thoughts came flooding into her mind, would he be a good man? Yes, it's the father's choice so he will be good -

she consoled herself. Would he be polite or as shy as herself or would be rude and straightforward? Does he have a beard or would he be clean shaved? Will he be tall or short, fat or lean and will he like her? Is she beautiful enough to be with him? What if he does not like her? - Will he leave her - she will go to her house or stay at her husband's place? All these weird, out-of-the-world thoughts were running through her mind and suddenly she heard a crackling noise as if someone had opened the door and she quickly pulled her veil down to her shoulders, making her face hidden.

Her husband - Bikram entered the room where Parvati was sitting in a maroon bridal outfit and her hands were shaking with nervousness. Bikram was tall, wheatish complexion, and clean shaved. He gently came and sat on the other corner of the bed. As he sat, Parvati was trembling with anxiety and her heartbeat has grown faster than ever. Bikram did not look at her but Parvati peeped through her veil and all she saw was the back of Bikram. After a dead silence of nearly 20-30 minutes, Bikram choose to speak first but the words that came afterward from his mouth shattered all the dreams of Parvati.

....

....

....

....

....

....

"I met young few years ago at my office, she is beautiful, educated and we love each other very. Her name is much Kamini and when I proposed to her for marriage, neither of

our families agreed as she was from a different caste, and then my family forced me to marry you. I am sorry, but Kamini is the only woman I love and who will live in my heart forever and I did this marriage only because of my family's continuous pressure, however, you will be my wife for the rest of my life and I will definitely honor and respect that but I cannot love you ever in this life."

After saying all these things to Parvati, Bikram choose the window side of the bed and slept saying - *it's getting too late and we should probably rest, need to wake up early*. While Bikram slept in a deep sleep, Parvati was still trying to figure out what just happened, how to react, what to say, whom to say, and what to do.

There was a deep silence that night, however, Parvati cried and cried all night putting a pillow over her head so that the sound of her cries shall not disturb Bikram's sleep. The next morning, Parvati woke up as a dutiful daughter-in-law, greeted everyone with a smile and touched their feet to get blessings, did all the household chores, and at night she was a dutiful wife. She knew as she was taught that she is now married which means good or bad, health or sickness, rich or poorer, she had to stay with this person for her entire life and it's her responsibility to make him happy and be an obedient wife.

A part of Parvati believed that it might be possible that men are like that and she is a good and loving person and probably one day Bikram would probably see this goodness and feel the same for her and love her.

A few days after the wedding, Bikram was leaving for the

city to resume his work and he decided to take Parvati along with him. With the dying spring, something also died inside Parvati, it was a pain she never, something she cannot tell anyone or something that no one understands. And with the rise of Summer, as decided, Parvati and Bikram touched the feet of all elders, took their blessings, and started their trip to the city. She was sitting on the window side of the bus with her husband, but it was different this time. She saw outside and there was nature, mountains, and waterfalls but her eyes were on the sky and all she could think is at least those birds can fly.

As the bus was moving and they came nearer and nearer to the city, Parvati did not have a single idea that she is unraveling a new chapter of her journey and this was just a start.

II

City Lights

After 6-7 hours, the bus reached its depot. Boy, there are lots of people. For the first time in her life, Parvati was witnessing such a crowd. People are running here and there, a few are even sleeping on the floor, there were refreshment counters and huge luggage and so many busses. Parvati got scared seeing so all this. The weather was also not pleasant, it was hot and sweaty and now, miles away from every person she ever knew in a totally unknown city, Bikram was her only hope and the only person she can count on.

The 1980s was the time when phone calls were not as cheap as today and since no one had a phone in the village so all the conversations were done through letters. Parvati used to write letters to her family but never mentioned anything regarding the most awkward revelation done by Bikram on the first night after her marriage. She did not want her family to be worried or especially blame her father for his choice. Moreover, what will she complain about, that she is not loved by her husband, love was something that was not in the dictionary at that time, all that was accepted by society was respect. And on what earth do we think her parents will understand this. Everyone saw a beautiful social image of Bikram and Parvati, which is accepted and honored by society. And no doubt Bikram was a responsible husband even though his feelings were cold toward Parvati so basically there was nothing to complain about.

Parvati tried really hard, every day, every moment, to make Bikram feel loved and happy as if it was her duty to make him happy. She forgets how she feels and her only focus is that Bikram is happy and content. Every morning, she woke up at 5 AM, make delicious breakfast, cleans the house, and then in the evening prepares a variety of mouthwatering food for dinner and then waits every night for Bikram to come home. She decorates the dining table and serves the dinner in the casserole so that it does not get cold get, then she goes outside to the balcony and her glittering innocent eyes were on the road, to see if he can get a glimpse of Bikram's return from the office. Sometimes it's 10 or 11 or 12 at night and her lonely eyes were still finding him but as soon as he notices Bikram at the corner of the street, slowly walking down towards the house, she rushes back inside and reheats all the food so that it is hot when served to Bikram. After a few minutes, the doorbell rings and she excitedly rushes toward the door only to find out he is drunk. But patiently, she welcomes him inside the house and goes rushing to the kitchen to get a chilled glass of water. She politely asks him to have dinner and serves all the dishes on his plate. Bikram ate dinner and walked toward the bedroom and laid down for sleep. He neither complements Parvati for such good food nor bothers himself to sit down with her few minutes to talk. Bikram never bothered himself to even ask if Parvati had his meal. Every day, she expects Bikram will spend time with her, and every day she is just cleaning the plates after dinner and eating the leftovers.

Seeing this cold and distant behavior even after all her continuous efforts, Parvati felt bad and moreover lonely and she cried all night in silence while Bikram was drunk and asleep. Tears rolled down and the pillow where her head was resting got a huge wet spot. The tears were uncontrollable and so was her mind which was running here and there and in all directions, trying to think about what wrong she had ever done and why there is no love in her fate. Her mind was thinking about every aspect - Was she not a good person? Is it her Karma of previous life that she is repaying now? Are all men like this only? Isn't she attractive enough? And much more. She cried herself to sleep with the hope that the next morning will be different and she will be appreciated, complimented and her husband will start loving her.

But unlike every morning, this morning was no different. She tried making small talk, tried much harder than yesterday to befriend her own husband but all in vain, there was simply no compassion or affection from Bikram's side. All she got is a tired, drunk man, murmuring about his old girlfriend in his sleep.

Soon after a few months, Parvati was expecting and she thought that this would be the seed of love that will grow and connect her and Bikram, Bikram took good care of Parvati while she was pregnant with their first child. As the doctor advised, Parvati go for walks, though Bikram never accompanied her, but, at home, he does talk with Parvati. Get her healthy food and take her to the doctor for regular checks. Unfortunately, all this happiness for Parvati was short-lived as destiny had some different plans for her. As it was their first child and there was no one in the city to look after her, Bikram's family pressurized him to take their daughter-in-law back to their house as there would be plenty of people to help her in this phase of life and Bikram too agreed. They took a bus back to their village while she was approximately 7-8 months pregnant and before reaching their stop, she complained about a nerve-wracking pain in her abdomen. As soon as the bus stopped, Bikram rushed her to a nearby hospital which was also 1-2 hours away and the doctors confirmed that she had a miscarriage.

Listening to those words coming from the doctor's mouth, Parvati got stunned and so as Bikram. They lost their first child and something was lost in Parvati that day. Maybe the hope. The hope of a happy family. The hope of love.

They came back to the city after a few days and everything was back as it was previously. The cold, distant, and drunk Bikram and a constant reminder that he still loves Kamini. Parvati started to curse her fate every day for the next one year until she was blessed with a beautiful daughter and now she has a reason to live, laugh, and love.

III

An Angel From Heaven

Parvati always loves to do gardening, she planted a few green chilies in her roof garden as the monsoon season was nearby. Bikram took a month's leave from the office to take care of Parvati as her due date was also nearby. And that day, with the start of the monsoon, it rained heavily and all the green chilies blossomed but that was still the second-best thing. A little angel was sent from heaven and the family was the first time in the years was so happy and together. Bikram took her little daughter in his arms and literally cried with happiness. He was was so happy that day, that he distributed sweets to the entire hospital. He helped Parvati and even started coming home early, talk to Parvati and play with his little daughter.

Bikram loved his daughter so much that Parvati as if this tiny little angel was sent from heaven to sort everything bad and sow the seeds of love in their heart. Parvati was determined that she will change everything wrong in her life and hoped that someday Bikram might have some love for her as well. And, before we go any further, till now you must assume that Bikram was not a good man. I would like to clarify that Bikram was a hardworking, helpful and responsible man. He cares for everyone around him, he was polite, friendly and on good days, was loving as well but when it comes to Parvati his feelings were cold. It might be because he has experienced the love before and it was not the same with Parvati. Also, deep down, he might know that he got a loving and caring wife at home who will be there no matter what. She was always an option to him because he knew she will neither complain nor had the nerve to leave. She will suffer in silence but never put dirt on him. And that was true, she cared too much that he never realized her true value.

After their first daughter- Tamanna, things seem better between Parvati and Bikram. Bikram, like said, earlier was much attached to their firstborn and also overly protective of her. As the years passed till the end, his over-protectiveness became the reason for destroying all the goodness and innocence of not only the childhood of their kids but affected Parvati in an extremely negative manner killing all the little hopes in her forever.

They say if you want an angel you need to create heaven as angels don't live in hell and if you keep them in hell, they get evolved and will no longer be an angel. The statement stands correct as you may give blame to angels for becoming a monster but it was the hell that took away the innocence and becoming a monster is the worst you can imagine and they do not have a happy ending until god revives them but in this, there was no god.

IV

The Summer Of 92

It's almost 2 decades since Parvati was born in this beautiful world, and has seen most of her life-changing events. Yes, she is no longer that innocent young girl who tries to catch butterflies in her garden. Now she is a daughter-in-law, wife, and mother. So many things changed in these two decades - ups and downs and today she is again in the same hospital after 2 years since Tamanna was born, eager to welcome her second child. It was a bright summer afternoon in June'92 when Parvati went into labor. The doctor was in her lunch break when suddenly she felt pain. Bikram rushed to call the doctor and nearly after 1-2 hours, Parvati delivered her second daughter - Kanak.

The doctor came and said, "*Congratulations, you are blessed with a daughter*", but it's still the 90s and people are encouraged to have a boy child rather than two girls in a middle-class household. Girls are still treated as a liability. However, Bikram was happy but not as attached as he was to their firstborn. When Kanak was born, they were already experienced with a lot of things, and hence it was easy to handle a second child. The news was delivered to the other family elders in the village, however, the reaction was not what Parvati expected. They made her feel as if why they have a second girl child and they should try for a boy next. It though broke the heart of Parvati but she knew how special these girls are to her. Anyway, she is living in the city and does not have to bother herself with this negativity on daily basis and just wanted to focus on her own family - Bikram and the girls.

Parvati and Bikram were normal middle-class people and worked very hard to live a respectable life thus Parvati decided that she did not want any more children in hope that one day she will have a boy. She knew that having half a dozen kids in hope of a boy is not a smart choice and, therefore, she gathered all her courage and said to Bikram, "*I do not want any more children. I don't care if I have a boy or a girl. We cannot afford to have more kids and thus we will raise our daughters like boys only. We will give them a good education, independence, love, fulfill their dreams and goals and raise them with all our available resources rather than having so many children and none of them are paid proper attention.*"

For the first time I believe, Parvati stood for what she wanted for her, it might be her love for her kids that she took a stand in front of Bikram and he too agreed and respected Parvati's decision and happily underwent vasectomy surgery.

Now, with two little kids, Parvati was busy with their upbringing but in the meantime, she also showed interest in learning sewing and getting more education little did she know that this interest might take away the little happiness that just started growing between Parvati and Bikram.

One day, after Bikram came back from the office, Parvati already tucked the kids in their beds and served the hot delicious food on the dining table. While Bikram was taking small bites of his food, Parvati tried making some small talk and after dragging the conversation here and there for 15-20 minutes she finally got to the point, "*I want to study. I want to go to college and get a degree. Also, I did some research and found a Fashion Institute nearby. I really want to learn the designing and stitching.*" Those words do not seem to go great with Bikram. He did not say anything at first but this thing touched his male ego. According to him, how can a woman go out of the house and be more educated than him? How can she be independent?

Now, while writing the past, I think about this, and I understand why he was against it because deep down there is a fear in his heart. He feared that if Parvati would be independent then why the hell would she be going to live with Bikram? Why is she will going to tolerate his disrespectful and hurting behavior? The best thing is to destroy the seed before growing. This new face of Bikram was about to come out in front of Parvati - egoistic, jealous, dominating, and mentally traumatizing.

That night, at the dinner table, Bikram showed nothing much of a disagreement or discomfort with Parvati's idea and they slept later on. The real game started, the following morning, he went to the office as every day and Parvati went to her new school. But that night was long, very long. She kept waiting for Bikram and at least when he showed up later than midnight. He was drunk like before. He cannot even stand and cannot even eat without creating a mess and then went to bed. The next morning, Parvati kept asking if something is bothering him but he did not say anything. He was just mute as if he do not want to talk to Parvati at all and so as the kids. The kids happily went to their father, but he did not bother to even talk to them and then just angrily replied *go away and do some work rather than just hanging around.* It was odd for Parvati to see disrespecting her children but she did not say anything and took her kids to another room and ask to play there.

Days and months passed like this, every day he is drunk and chooses not to talk to anyone, and all the time he is at home he is just watching television. Parvati did not get what he is struggling with. She tried to make all her efforts but everything goes in vain. When Bikram meets people outside, he was just fine and smiling in front of them and happy to make conversations but it's just the three of them in the house that he does not want to talk to and Parvati is not understanding the reason for this. One day, when waiting for Bikram, she started analyzing when it started to happen and it took her to the night when she asked Bikram for getting an education. Now, everything makes sense to her. The problem is not herself or her kids. It's her education that he cannot deny but it seems that he does not want her to pursue her dreams. It was again a hard choice in front of Parvati - to take education at the stake of her family or just stay at home in peace. She cried and cried and her kids standing at the corner of the door got a glimpse of their crying mother. They were too young to understand the reason but seeing their mother cry made them deeply sad and as soon the doorbell rang, they rushed to bed - might be scared of their father or just don't want their parents to know that they know what is happening.

Parvati served food and calmly told Bikram that "*if he does not want her to go to school she will not go but please don't come home drunk every night, and don't ignore me and your own kids. They want their father. It is okay with me that you cannot love me but what is their fault for all this? They are innocent and don't know anything. They deserve their father's love, care, and attention. I will do what makes you happy but please don't give us this cold treatment*", she cried uncontrollably.

The next morning, Bikram's behavior was better than before and he started talking to the kids and Parvati. Heartbroken Parvati gave up her dreams but it was just a matter of a few days before Bikram's behavior changed again. He started to come drunk again and started to have problems with everything. Occasional small disagreements were always there between the couple but these disagreements have taken a new turn i.e. fights. Became more frequent along with the unnecessary verbal abuse.

She now knows that there is no pleasing him therefore she secretly joined the fashion designing course once the children joined the school. Bikram leaves in the morning for the office and Parvati took the children to school and from there she went to her classes. She returns in the afternoon, cooks lunch for the children, and then goes to the school to pick them up. Everything was going smoothly and the children also knew about this but never told their father anything as they knew that this may lead to a fight between their parents and that was the last thing they ever wanted, and moreover, they were happy to see their mother happy and follow her dreams. Parvati was one of the most hardworking and dedicated students in her batch and was always praised for her work and concepts. But to be perfect, she needs to practice.

On her marriage, as a gift, she was given a sewing machine by her parents, which was just lying somewhere in the house for the past few years, but now she had a chance to take it out and work on it. She started practicing on that machine but still getting cloth pieces for practice was a challenge as this might reveal this secret and Bikram would be disappointed and angry, so she used old newspapers in place of cloth pieces to practice designing clothes as this won't grab Bikram's attention.

One day, Bikram when searching for something came across books about Parvati and came to know that she was taking classes and a huge fight broke out between them where enraged Bikram put wrongful allegations on Parvati so that she quit the class out of guilt that she upset her husband and that is exactly what happened. She quit the class thinking it was her fault that she joined the class against Bikram's wish and as a dutiful wife she should not disobey her husband and do whatever makes him happy and this is the only way to avoid any fights.

Since she already learned almost everything before quitting, she continued her practice at home and started to sew clothes for others to earn some money for her savings and with kids going to school, she was able to educate herself along with her children.

Parvati always wished and does things that make Bikram

happy with the only hope that he won't fight with her, will not abuse her, will not be distant with their kids but she never knew that Bikram wants a puppet. He wants to control every aspect of the life of Parvati as well as the kids. She never knew that Bikram will never be happy with her or the kids because somewhere he only thinks they are his responsibility but not the love. He was a man who only love people for his own convenience and making such a person happy is not only difficult but impossible as they shall find one way or another to blame.

V

1st Attempt

Every person has some sort of limits and they cannot hold beyond that limit. Although with time and experience this limit does grow, but, this was indeed new for Parvati. She came from a house where no one even talks to each other in loud voice, everyone is respected in the family and even if their parents are angry with each other, they do not fight or use foul language. That was the kind of home that Parvati grew up so she expected the same from her partner as well. But, after years of living with Bikram, her expectations were hurt but she could not understand or she does not want to understand the harsh reality of life and people.

With time Bikram grew distant from Parvati and their children. He always comes home fully drunk and abuses Parvati and the kids. He continuously pulls his tantrums to make Parvati realize that her work is not appreciated, she is not a good wife and mother and he is upset to even see her around but in reality, he never wants Parvati to be independent.

Parvati cries every day and being a stupid Indian wife, she always felt as if she was the reason for her husband's drinking habits and since the abuse was mostly verbal rather than physical so she did not say anything. She thinks, he is abusing her because he is drunk and otherwise he would not do this. She just cries for her fate and prays to get this over and hopes this should be the last day and everything will be good the next morning as he will be sober. The kids saw their mother crying every day, all night while the father passed unconsciously. Their innocent eyes had so many questions but they were too afraid to talk.

There was no way to get rid of this situation as Bikram finds one way or another to blame Parvati for his drinking and then abusing her that she is not a good wife and Parvati has to live with all this because of the society, her family and for her children.

Bikram leaves for the office in the morning and usually, he comes home late at night and is drunk so Parvati makes the kids sleep so that they should not be a part of the daily drama. But when Bikram comes it was all noisy as he used to shout and fight unnecessarily.

Kanak does not have a deep sleep and usually gets up and hears everything and sees her mother crying every night from a small hole in her blanket but was too afraid to get her head out of that sheet or say anything as if she was paralyzed with fear and therefore, Parvati never realized that the kids already know about all this and in the morning when Bikram left for office and mother wakes up the children, they both greeted each other as if nothing happened in night and children did not have the nerve to ask and also they do not want their mother to be embarrassed in front of them and also not to remember the horrifying nights.

Then one day, Parvati was completely broken, she do not know how to end her daily sufferings. She found herself in a box with no way. She was so disheartened and broken that to get rid of this daily nuisance, Parvati decided to end her life.

Only if it was that easy!

There is a known saying that "*Waqt se pehle aur kismat se jyada kisi ko kuch nahi milta*" [*You cannot get anything before time and beyond your destiny*]. And it seems correct in this situation. Parvati was fed up and wanted to end it for all, but it seems like destiny had some other plans for her. When Bikram went to his room after dinner, Parvati did not follow him which made him a little curious he went to the kitchen and saw Parvati vomiting badly. As he rushed towards her, he found a bottle of poison near the kitchen door. She did all the vomiting and was stable. All the poison was out of her system but she was still weak. The next day, Bikram took her to the hospital and said that she was not feeling well. The doctor gave her medications and after a few days, she was in good health. Her kids did not have much idea what happened or anything, and the father told her mother is ill and needed rest for a few days.

Bikram took care of Parvati when she was on bed rest and also apologized for his behavior and said, "*Parvati, promise me that you will never do such thing again. I am sorry. It's because of alcohol that I became this monster. I am really sorry."*

Parvati: But if you are not happy with me you can leave me and I do not want to be a burden in your life.

Bikram: Please don't say that. You are my wife. [sobbing continues] I promise, I will never drink alcohol again.

Parvati thought that Bikram has genuinely changed and become a better person and he won't drink as well. Now Bikram came home early, he talks to Parvati, plays, and have fun with their daughters.

Things were okay for a few days or might be for a few months but expecting happiness for a long time was just a myth in this household. They say the habits can be changed or evolved with time but this is not a habit, this is who he is - a man who does not respect others, a man who thinks that he is always right, a man to whom his own happiness matters, a man who likes throwing tantrums and who may like people around him making a fuss about him only. This is not a habit. This is the person, maybe how he is raised, maybe how he had seen the things around him. I try to think sometimes about this story from the point of view of Bikram, and why was like that. He had his own struggles as a child but when he got a loving family why he is so cold towards them. Was alcohol the only issue? Or his mind? Or is there anything we do not know? We see him as a selfish person but by the end, you may guess or it would still be complicated.

VI

The Ugly Truth

Despite everything, Parvati never complained to anyone that she was not happy. Every day seems to be a burden. But her values were higher than her misery. This was a person, his family has chosen and she cannot insult the decision of her family by complaining about it.

One summer, Parvati's younger brother's marriage was fixed and hence she went alone to her parent's house to be a part of the wedding function as summer vacations haven't started yet, and thus Bikram have to stay with the children for their school and they decided to join Parvati a few weeks later.

Though it was the summer season the nights were cold and breezy. One night, after dinner, Parvati was taking after-dinner walks in her garden with her mother when. Her mother asked about her household and Bikram and she suddenly felt a wave of emotion. She does not want her parents to be worried about her but she cannot live with this burden and thus she broke down in front of her mother and did mention a few things that Bikram drinks a lot and shouts and fights with her for no good reason. She told her she felt as if she is not needed but her mother said, [in a very calm and polite tone] "*Every girl has her own home which is her husband's place. If both of you will fight then there is never a solution for a thing. You should do compromise sometimes. Everyone does compromises. No one is perfect and men do have more responsibilities than women so sometimes they snap, but as a wife and a woman, it is your duty to keep the family together no matter what. I know it's your life and your household and disagreements happen in every household but you should always remember the image of your parents, in-laws, and husband and respect them and should not bother yourself with these things rather you can focus on your children and husband and do what makes him happy. Once a day or another he will see the goodness in you and come to you and your father must have seen something in that guy as he won't just marry you off to anyone. Do not overthink everything. Everything will be good. You are blessed with your children and you may try to have a son as it is very important to have a son*".

Listening to these words of her mother, Parvati knew that she would not be getting any support from her own family with whom she spent 17 years of her life and they do not understand their own daughter at all. It was heartbreaking for her and she got nothing but disappointment from them. If these words are said by someone else it might not bother her much but she does have some expectations from her family. That day she decided that she cannot quit, she needs to be there, she needs to live for her daughters and make them stand on their own feet so that they will not become another Parvati, they do not have to depend on anyone and can live a life of pride and on their own terms.

Being a person of the 21st century, I never understand what was stopping Parvati from leaving Bikram. Why does she want to be with such a person who neither respects nor loves her? Fortunately, there is no need to guess the answer as Parvati here because she told the answer but I will let you know about it when the time is right.

So, moving on with the story, years passed but nothing changed, her kids are now in school. I believe they are in the 3rd and 5th class. The behavior of Bikram did not change and one day Bikram introduced his family to a young girl and said she works in her office. He said to the kids she is your new mom, Parvati did not react and just took this as a joke in front of the children but yes, of course, she felt bad, years after years one or another girl was introduced and Parvati never said anything.

Despite endless efforts from Parvati, things did not get better and we can say it was now worsened. Bikram returns from the office, he does not even talk to Parvati or the kids, just drinks and sleeps. Parvati understands that he was busy but on the other hand he talks for hours with others on the phone or other people. It was just his family that had every problem as if he does not want to even see them.

Parvati always felt bad but never said anything as she did not have any proof and her values did not let her suspect or blame her husband also a part of Parvati always believed that he may tease her, he may not talk to her, he may abuse her, he may not love her but he is a good man and will never betray her trust.

I really do not understand what kind of society we live in where a man does everything a human is capable of and still be respected and a woman has to compromise on everything and still she is the one who is always blamed for anything wrong. What is her fault? That she is a woman. Why do we always forget that a woman is capable of unconditional love, respect, and forgiveness? She understands everything, she understands the positive things in the most negative situations. She may be independent or dependent but she will not give up. Because she is a woman. She will never give up and will try till her last breath to make everything correct. Everyone tries to break her but she will fight and will stand right by you no matter what. That is a woman. But she has a limit, might be more but yes there is a limit. Yes, she is soft-hearted, she will forgive and even forget but she is not dumb. She gives numerous chances because she is a woman. Even though it kills her but she will make you smile, because she is a woman. But still, she is treated like nothing because she is a woman.

Why a girl is not a responsibility of her family after marriage? She is just going to another house but you are the one who brought her into this world. She never said asked you to have unprotected sex, she did not ask you to give her life but once you gave birth to that human it is 100% your responsibility. How a mother forgets that pain of 9 months, how a brother forgets the Rakhi vows to protect her sister from any evil, how the sisters forget their playful time together, and how a father forgets that she is a part of him as well. All they care about is the society, what they will think, and what will they say and no one dares to ask how she feels, what she wants, and what she thinks. Yes, the questions should be changed and not in quotes or in an essay writing competition but in the mind. Scientists say that humans have brains, they are better than every living organism but are they really better?

How things turned out for Parvati later in this story might have not resulted in that way only if someone would have supported her initially. She was never a liability, she was a daughter, a wonderful, dutiful daughter who no matter what, and how much she suffered but stayed with Bikram till her last breath and never put a single stain on Bikram's identity or ever questioned or blamed her family. So much sacrifice and so much love, I guess a woman can only have.

As we continue the story, I would like to let you know that this is not a happy ending, this is a story of how three lives were destroyed forever and that destruction was not overnight but the years and years of suffering. The reason behind this destruction was also one person but the whole community/society. And there are many Parvati's out there who struggle, suffer, and ultimately give up.

VII

The 2nd Attempt

The children are now in their teens and I sometimes wonder how all those years passed. Things are never better and with time for none of them. The only time when the family actually enjoy was when Bikram was gone to his office or out of the station. In his presence, everyone needs to talk less, behave the way he wanted, do whatever he says, and if the things are not his way he fights with Parvati and abuses their children. But when he is not around, the kids and Parvati does have fun, they play games, they go to the park and even Parvati entertains the kids with her childhood stories.

Everyone was attempting to keep the decorum of the house maintained as if they were in jail as one thing were wrong and Bikram will lose his control one day, Parvati came to know that his father died due to a long illness. She was at home when the kids came from school and it was unusual for them to see Bikram at that time in the house.

Bikram: You guys freshen up and have food.

Kanak: Where is the mother?

Bikram: She is inside. Not feeling well.

Kanak: [changed clothes and went to her mother] Mom what happened?

Bikram: Your grandfather died and we need to go to their place. We are going right away so take care of yourself.

Kanak and Tamanna: Okay, we will take care.

A few days later, Bikram and Parvati arrived back after all the funeral rituals were completed. Parvati was sad and broken while Bikram seem distant. There was something going on in his mind but right now Parvati was not in the mood to look after him when she herself was in the most vulnerable phase. A month passed while Bikram was still not talking to anyone. Every day he comes back from the office and does not talk to anyone and sits in his room and drinks alcohol till he passed out. Seeing all these things at the time when Parvati needed him the most breaks her heart. He does not have any empathy or anything and one day Parvati decided to talk to him.

Parvati: I am seeing this for the past one and a half months. I do not know what I have done, or why you are upset with me. But why you are giving yourself pain. This alcohol is killing you. Please tell me what I have done?

Bikram: [fully drunk] I hate you. You don't deserve me. You are not a good woman because at the funeral you were crying on your sister's husband's shoulder. What were you trying to show everyone that I am a bad husband. And how dare you to lean on another man's shoulder.

Parvati: My dad just died and I didn't realize who was there and whose shoulder was it. Also, my sister's husband is elder to me and we always treated them like we treat our father. How can you be so cruel to say and blame me for such a thing?

Parvati kept crying and Bikram was outraged and he kept on abusing her and blaming her for the things he made up in his mind and then he passed out as he drank a lot of alcohol.

Kids were in the other room but they did not have the courage to say anything. It was extremely late in the night and they did not know but they fell asleep. Although after some time, may like an hour or so there were again some noises but these were different. Kanak peeped from her sheets and saw that his uncle [mother's brother who lived nearby] came home and he and dad were getting fresh water and there was no voice of Parvati. Something seemed odd about all this and slowly Kanak gathered all the courage and came out of her sheets and went ahead to the dining room area just to see that her mother was lying and vomiting on the floor. She came closer and said, "*Mother, what happened*" her mother looked at her with her dizzy eyes and said everything is fine and then her uncle asked her to leave and everything is fine.

The next morning, the kids went to the school while their mother was still taking a rest, and as they came back, Kanak and Tamanna went to see their mom and stand at a distance.

Parvati: Kanak and Tamanna, come here and pulled her hand forward.

Kanak and Tamanna: Came quietly and sat beside their mother.

{they both sat down and hugged their mother from the side and snuggled}

Parvati: Are you angry with me. You know I love you both very much. I am sorry for taking such a step. I promise that this will never happen again. I will not leave you ever. [tears fell across her cheeks]

Kanak and Tamanna: [still processing what has happened and do not know what to say they just hugged their mother tightly as if they will never let her go although their hearts were broken by their mother's action but still they were happy to see that their mother was fine] We love you so much.

VIII

Separate Roads

Years passed and passed and things did not change. Kids are also now all grown up and working in their respective fields. It was a late winter evening when Kanak arrived from the office. Parvati opened the door as usual but something was unusual about that evening. Her eyes were red as if she had been crying for hours. Kanak entered the house and went to her room and after a few minutes, Parvati came to her.

Parvati closed the door and said, "Kanak, I want to tell you something".

Kanak: Yes, what happened?

Parvati: Your father is having an affair. [in a sobbing voice]

Kanak: [replied laughing] Mom you are thinking anything. That can't be true. He must be joking around.

Parvati: [in a deep sobbing tone while tears started to drop down her cheeks] I am not joking. It's true.

[Serious tense silence]

Kanak: Why are you saying that? What happened?

Parvati: Last night when I went to the bedroom to ask your father to join us for dinner. I heard him talking to someone, saying, "*I really love you. I want to be with you only. You are the only one who understands me. I am stuck with these people but my heart belongs to you.*" I did not say anything that time and as soon as he saw me he disconnected the call. But, at night when he was asleep I was still thinking about the same, and something did not feel right so I went ahead and checked his phone. There were so many text messages and pictures of him with another woman. I secretly took his phone number and tried calling her this morning but when she listened to my voice she disconnected my call and blocked me.

[Parvati crying]

Kanak: Give me the number. Let me call her and check what is happening?

Kanak dialed that number from her phone and a woman picked up the call but as soon as Kanak said I am Bikram's daughter, she disconnected the call and then blocked her. Kanak did not know what to say to her mother at that time but calmly said let's talk to papa and sort this out and clear the things. There is no point in crying so be patient and let him come from the office.

A few hours later Bikram arrived and he went straight to his bedroom and laid down and did not talk to anyone. While Parvati waited and waited for him to come and talk but seeing this behavior was unacceptable. Parvati and Kanak went to Bikram's room and

Kanak said: Mom saw the messages and she called and I too called that woman. Who is she?

Bikram: She is a friend. And why did you even call her, if you want something you should ask me.

Kanak: But why then did she blocks us and was too worried to even talk to us?

Bikram: You mind your own business and I don't want to talk to you. You all are pathetic and u don't deserve an answer. [in a loud angry voice]

Kanak: Okay, so what do you want? Do you want us in your lives?

Bikram: You should all get lost. I do not want anyone in my life. [getting extremely loud and aggressive]

Kanak: You do not want us in your life?

Bikram: I don't want anyone in my life. You all have ruined my life and I am well off without you.

Kanak: Now, I am asking you the third time, do you want me, mother, and Tamanna in your life or not. [a little heavy voice]

Bikram: No I do not want you three in my life. Now go.

Kanak: Okay. Thank you for confirming.

Kanak left the room and Parvati followed her. They went to Kanak's room and Parvati was crying while Kanak had to be strong for her mother. She said, "*we don't want this man if he does not want us. We can go somewhere else and live a peaceful life. Please give him a divorce. You are better off without him. And this man can be your husband but he is not my father anymore. You may forgive him after a few days when he will come back to you but I cannot forget this thing my entire life.*"

Days passed and the situation was still the same, where Bikram was not talking to anyone in the house. Kids went to the office and came home in the evening while Parvati was in the house the whole day and literally dying inside every day.

One day, Tamanna came home and she was drunk which infuriated Parvati and she slapped her. Later that night Parvati came to Kanak while she was doing some office work and said in a sobbing tone, "*Kanak, your father has broken my expectation at every single point. Just when I believe that he will be a better husband, he crushes my trust so hard, and now your sister. I trust her with everything and she is just doing the same as your father. I cannot take it anymore. I do not want to leave you with these people. Kanak, will you die with me after which they will get to know what they have lost.*"

Kanak: Death is not a lesson and you never know that our death will be a lesson for them or they shall get the freedom to do whatever they want. Also, why do we die? We have suffered enough. We too deserve a happy life?

[Kanak continues]

I got a job in another city and now I intend to move there, I cannot live here with this man when he clearly said he does not want us. Mom, come with me. We will leave them and we will start a new life. A life of freedom and happiness. You do not have to listen or think about anyone, just be selfish for once and think about yourself. Just come with me and live the life you deserve.

Parvati: I cannot. [in a low tone] He is my husband and she is my daughter. I cannot leave them. What will society think? My parents told me that we have sent you as a bride to this house and now only your body will leave this house.

Kanak: Those people and those societies are never around when you need them. Why do you even think of them?

Parvati: Kanak, if you want to go then go but I cannot go with you.

[a long silence]

After a few days, Kanak went to the new city and took the new job. though she was concerned about her mother she cannot go back to that place again or even talk to her father. She choose herself, she was selfish, she tried to help her mother but as they say, people who cannot help themselves even God cannot help them and that is true here.

A few months later, Parvati told Kanak that she has forgiven his father and they have reconciled but it was not unusual news seeing the past experiences. Bikram misbehaves, gives cold treatment for days, and then one day he came over drunk and apologizes and Parvati forgiveness. But Kanak was determined that no matter what she will not be going to let her family members ruin her life anymore and no amount of forgiveness will ever heal the wounds her family gave her in these 25 years.

IX

A Day Beofre

Seven months passed and Bikram and Kanak were still not on talking terms. She talks to Parvati on the phone, but she has shut Bikram out of his life and never understands why Parvati forgave him. But as her mother said, "*Whatever happens between a husband and wife it's their life and choice, and being a child you cannot disrespect your father.*" So, not being disrespectful toward her father Kanak choose to stay away from home if that would make everything good and her mother will be at peace.

Things were fine between Parvati and Bikram as they found a suitable match for their elder daughter and were occupied with tasks for the upcoming winter wedding. She did forgive her daughter for drinking but that was mostly because she wanted to wed her off and do not want any reason that might hamper the peace of the house.

She did a compromise for her happiness. But compromises cannot last long if they are done from one side only. You can not live happily as living is never a compromise. Happiness is a choice and life is a decision.

Even though things were better between Parvati and Bikram but that did not keep away Bikram from his drinking habits. One day, on a weekend, when Tamanna went out with her friends, she said she will return by evening, however, it was getting late and late at night and she called and said she had a flat. Bikram was outraged and kept n drinking alcohol and abusing and cursing Parvati. Parvati was on the other hand terrified about her child as well as Bikram.

Later that night at around 2 AM, Kanak's phone rang,

Kanak: Hi mom, you have not slept yet?

Parvati: No, were you sleeping?

Kanak: No, not exactly. What happened?

Parvati: [in a slow and sobbing tone] Tamanna went out with her friends but hasn't come back home yet. Your dad is drunk and passed out. I don't know what to do. If he wakes up, he will be extremely angry. I don't know why she doesn't understand this. Her phone is also off. I am very afraid and hope nothing bad had happened.

Kanak: [in a consoling voice] Mom, I do not know what to say but why do you bother yourself. They will never change. Her phone is off, what can I do. You should go and get some sleep, her battery probably died and she would be okay and will be back. If papa gets up you just lie to him that she was near my house and thus she did a sleepover at my place and her battery died and I forgot to tell. We will wait for her call and I will try calling her in case I get a hold of her. Please don't cry and go and sleep. Everything will be fine.

Parvati: Okay, you take a rest. Bye.

Kanak: Bye. Take care.

The phone disconnected, however, neither Parvati slept nor Kanak. And after maybe half an hour, the phone rang again.

Parvati: Kanak, I got a call from the police station and they said Tamanna is there as they [Tamanna and her friends] were drinking alcohol in the car. [Crying uncontrollably] I don't know what to do. She got shame in our family and if your father will get to know about this, I am not sure what he will do. [sobbing continues]

Kanak: Mom, don't cry. Give me the number from which you got the call and I am coming home and we will go there and get her. Don't worry, everything will be fine.

Kanak dressed up, called on that number, and got the location. She went home, picked up her father and mother and they all went to the police station. After reaching there, they got Tamanna and a police person told them that it is okay to drink but not on road. Don't say anything or scold her.

While coming back, everyone was silent. Yeah, what was there to say. Parvati looked out of the window and cried while Bikram held his tears but was quiet. Soon they reached home and Bikram sat on the couch and turned on the television while Tamanna went straight to her room. Parvati went to the dining room and sat on the chair. Kanak followed her mother to the dining room.

Kanak: Mom, it is okay. It is not a big deal. Please forget about today.

Parvati: [crying] Why, she did do this?

Kanak: I don't know what to say but just leave them. Please don't bother yourself. I need to leave as I have an office in the evening.

Parvati: Can you stay?

Kanak: It's Monday and there is a lot of work and I cannot take an unplanned leave. I will come back on weekend.

Parvati: Kanak, please take care of yourself. I love you. I trust you with everything and I love you so much.

Kanak: I love you to mother, don't think about it. Everything will be fine.

She wiped her mother's tears from her hand and kissed her on the forehead and went to the drawing-room where she saw her father. She is seeing her after months.

Kanak: Papa, I am leaving. Take care of yourself and your mother. Everything will be fine. It's not a big deal.

Bikram: You are going? Okay, take care. Bye.

Kanak left the house and in the evening talked to her mother on call to check if she is fine.

Parvati was not crying that night, but she was thinking about all her mistakes. Her trust was crushed every single point of time by Bikram and Tamanna. *She loved both of them so much. A mother always has a special attachment to her firstborn, but she was also being betrayed by her. She does not have Bikram, she does not have Tamanna and she realized and regretted all her decisions and choices. She questioned her existence. She questioned her fate. She never felt so nothing in her life that she felt that day as if she died years ago when she was married and all these years it was only her body that was there. She did not have a soul left. She was not disappointed now with anyone. She was disappointed with herself and why she did not end everything right from the start. Why she has grown everything so far. Why she could not stand for herself. Why was she so weak. Why did she think of everyone when in the end there was no one to think about her.*

She was also a human and she had every right to live her life the way she wanted it. Why her right to life was taken away by everyone. Why she was never treated like a daughter, sister, wife, and mother. She did everything she can but why still she is disappointed. Is she really disappointed by everyone or she is disappointed in herself, for her own incapabilities as a human, for her own choices. and things go on and on in her mind.

X

One's End

It was an afternoon of initial Winter, approximately 2 PM when Kanak suddenly woke up, she felt a little heavy-hearted, with tears flowing down her cheeks. There was not a single reason but she feel like crying. After laying in her bed for almost 2 hours and crying, suddenly her alarm rang. It was 4 PM. She needs to get ready for the office but something felt strange about that afternoon. Yes, Parvati did not call her. Always at 4 PM, she used to call her and wake her up but not that day. She felt strange and tried calling her mother. The bell rang and rang but no one picked up. She thought, that maybe the mother was feeling low and was sleeping. Kanak got ready for the office and left. While traveling in the Metro with her friend, she seem a little distracted, and as soon as she reached her stop and was going downstairs from the platform, her phone rang.

After almost 10-11 months, Bikram was calling her. She saw the screen of her phone and saw the name "Papa Calling", she was sure that something was not right. She was nervous but picked up the call and said, "*Hi Papa! How are you?*"

From the other side, Bikram replied, "*Did you talk to your mother today? She is not picking up my call.*"

Kanak: *Yes, I called her this afternoon but she did not pick up the call.*

Bikram: *I am calling her since early afternoon and she is not picking up my call as well. [Bikram said sobbing] Your mother was upset, I am afraid that she must not have harmed herself.*

Kanak: *Have you tried calling Tamanna?*

Bikram: *Yes, She also did not pick up the call. [Sobbing continues] Kanak, I am sure that something bad happened.*

Kanak: *[in a consoling voice although she was terrified inside] Papa, don't think bad. Mummy must be out with friends for an evening walk. Ask the neighbor aunty to check the house.*

Kanak disconnects the call and boarded the office cab. She went to the office but her heart knew something bad happened. She was seeing her phone, again and again, to check if her father called or messaged her to give an update. And then suddenly the phone rang, her hands were shivering and she picked up her phone.

Bikram: *Kanak, come home.*

Kanak: *What happened?*

Bikram: *Your mother died. She died. She did suicide. [sobbing uncrontrollably] I asked your uncle [mother's bother] to go and check the house as she was not picking up the call. I am going home, please come home as early as you can.*

Kanak: *Don't cry. I am coming..........*

Kanak disconnected the call and went to her manager to ask for the leave for rest of the day due to some personal reason and booked a cab. There was a huge traffic jam and even after boarding the cab around 7 PM, she reached home at around 11 PM.

Her house was on the 4th floor and there was a huge crowd of people, media, and police around the house. As she went upstairs, one of the women came crying towards her and grabbed her tightly, and hugged her. Not only she but everyone present there was staring at Kanak while her father was being interrogated by police. The woman took her inside one of the bedrooms where there were a large number of women sitting and crying. Kanak was seeing everyone sobbing but not a single drop of tear came into her eyes as if all the emotions have gone when a police officer came and handed her a letter written by her mother to Kanak. She read it and asked where is she.

The police personnel replied they are in the adjacent room. Kanak asked if she can see them when suddenly one of her relatives said, "*Why do you want to see them. Leave it*". Kanak ignored her and went ahead to the room. She saw her mother hanging from the ceiling while her sister was in the bed - lifeless and blue. She hears the people and relatives and Bikram saying that "*Parvati was a nice woman and they do not know what has triggered her and why she took such a harsh step.*" And she went to the corner of the living room and said to one of the police lady, "*I need to tell something to the investigating officer.*"

Kanak went to the living room and said, "*I want to talk to you, however, I want everyone else to leave and only papa can stay.*" She told me everything that happen the day before. She only told what happened the day before as that was what she can think of at that time when was the triggering point. After that, the bodies were taken to the dining room. Kanak saw the lifeless bodies of her mother and sister while everyone was crying near her. She was all dry, not because she does not care, but because she knew that finally her mother can rest and she is in a better place and she does not need to see all those fake people.

Later that night, the bodies were taken to the morgue and there were still relatives coming to the house. Kanak was sitting in the same room where the bodies were found and rather than crying she was normal. The next day, after the end rituals, at home, she found the people, relatives, neighbors, and father either blaming Parvati or Tamanna. But that was enough.

"You do not have any right to blame anyone when you were there and did never help. It was not an overnight thing. Everyone present in the room knows exactly what she is going through for the last 30 years but none of you did have the spine to stand with her nor cared so there is no point in blaming those who have gone while the actual culprit is everyone here. There is no point in shedding these fake crocodile tears when you did nothing when she was alive. All she wanted was the emotional support of her family but all she got was excuses. All she wanted was the love of her husband but what she got was betrayal, all

she wanted was respect from her children but what she got was dishonor. It's easy to blame but it takes a lot of courage to take responsibility for anything and you cowards don't have that courage." Kanak said angrily and in a loud tone. After that, there was a pin drop silence.

Kanak for a moment took a glance at everyone around her and then the photo of her mother and sister and then in a heavy voice with watery eyes just said that she needs to leave right now as being around the people like all of these is extremely suffocating, seeing all these people crying is torture, and listening to their wise [the dumbest things] words makes her vomit and she opened the main door of her home and stomped away. She did not know that it was the last time she was ever standing in that house. She was seeing her house and her family for the last time. Everything was coming to an end. Yes, it was the end indeed and definitely not the happy ending. She never looked back but carried no regrets in her heart that day. She saw the freedom but there was a wound in her heart that might be filled one day but its print will remain forever.

XI

Another's Beginning

That day Kanak not only left the house, but she also made a choice. The choice is that she won't be like her mother. This world will not tell her what to do or what not to do. Her decision will her hers and those people who cannot stand her personality are more than welcome to leave. It is better to have no one than to live around a pile of garbage. She choose herself that day and promised to choose herself over and over again. She knew it will be difficult - She does not have a home, she does not have a family, she does not have relatives and she was alone in this world but now she is fearless and the strongest. She chooses her life on her terms. Life from now on would not be easy but there will be peace.

Kanak left the house that day and then started with her office to as not to bother herself anymore. But Bikram contact her every day and to her surprise not ask if she was okay but to make her feel sorry that how lonely he is. She asked her father to get over this and focus on other things, be a nice man, and stop drinking but all he does is cry and want to stay with her at her apartment. Kanak does not want to be rude and always politely refused the proposal of living together. She does not want to go into the mess her mother stayed in for 30 years. A year passed like this and her mother's death anniversary came. She has not seen her father since she left her home that day but she put herself together and went the home and there were lots of people. Her father said hello and she went into the house. Her father never came to talk to her or even greeted her properly. This broke her heart. All she ever wanted to listen to was Bikram to accept that he did wrong but he was happily putting blame on her sister which was beyond acceptance for Kanak.

After nearly 15-20 minutes, she just got up and walked away. This time the feeling was different. She did not feel that it was her home or they are the people she knew. It broke her heart but she never let people see her broken pieces.

A few days after that, she came to know that Bikram got married again. She called her father and this time he blamed Kanak for taking this step. "*You went and there was no one to look after me and therefore my family forced me to marry*", Bikram said crying.

Listening to his words, Kanak was stunned. He always gets a reason for his doings and she politely replied, "*I am happy for you that you choose your happiness. You were lonely while your whole family, friends, and relatives were right by your side. You blame me for leaving you but have you ever thought that how I was living, if I was dead or alive, if my health is fine. But it is fine. I am not so weak to put the blame game. You be happy with your partner and respect her and love her. But please do not contact me from now on. Whenever you call me, I live 25 years of my life all over again and they are not the happy moments. I think we are better off without each other. You have all my best wishes. I do not want anything from you, neither love nor money. You are starting a new life so do not make the same mistake this time. You are fortunate that God has given you a second chance to be with someone, don't ruin it. Bye......"*

Kanak disconnected the call and looked around at her empty apartment. She found a cigarette nearby and lit it up and with a blank expression on her face, she was looking out of the window as if nothing can hurt her anymore. She then picked up her phone and blocked Bikram from everywhere so that he shall not contact her anymore and crushed the cigarette bud and went to the washroom to freshen up for the office.

XII

The Blame Game

I believe it is the human coping mechanism to blame others. No one wants to take responsibility for anything wrong. And I am not surprised by this. Taking ownership of something wrong is a big choice. It may lead to guilt, regret, and self-disappointment. In order to live a guilt-free life, humans tend to forget the part they played. They forget they are not perfect and not only do they forget, they tend to put the blame on something else. Deep down, everyone knows when they are wrong and when they are right but accepting your mistakes does not make you small. It makes you grow as a better human and a respectable person in your own eyes.

There is no one to see you, the people you are surrounded by will be gone over the period of time, and no one will ever remember you after 50 years but still we humans tend to live a life for others and it's not that they do not want to accept, it's that they have not even realized. Whenever something bad or wrong happens, we try to put a shield around us and make ourselves believe that it's not our fault.

It's destiny or it's someone else's fault. Acceptance is the second stair but we do not even want to climb the first stair of realization. Sometimes, we know inside our heads but generally, we make a fake illusion around us. This happened with Bikram and Parvati's family as well.

The damage is done. People are gone but still, Bikram believed that it was Tamanna that this happened. He was so convinced with the fact that he just wanted to hear the same from Kanak which she always refused. All Kanak wanted was a heartfelt apology from Bikram but he cannot give the one. Kanak had proved but Bikram was too convinced that he had not played any role in it that he choose to not talk to Kanak rather than face her and apologize for his behavior.

But he was not the only one, there were Parvati's relatives, who initially blamed Tamanna and later blamed Bikram. They were vicious towards Bikram but have always neglected the part they all played. It was not the thing that happened overnight. It was Parvati's third attempt to kill herself and the difference is that she got succeeded this time. Her family always knew what she was going through, and how unhappy she is in her marriage. She also told her brothers and sister about Bikram's extramarital affair but all they had was "*You keep quiet for a few more months, once Tamanna will be married, we will sit and talk to Bikram*". Whom this poor Parvati can count on, she did not have the courage to leave Bikram and her family never supported her. She spend 30 years of her life in a toxic relationship and even having a family she was all alone. Those families never stood up for Parvati, neither when she was alive and not even after she died. They just found a way to blame others for their own incapabilities.

So far, what I personally learned was those who are gone are gone but people survive at the stake of everyone else. They are there till then the dirt is not on their plate but as soon as the tables are turned people vanish as if they have never existed.

XIII
The Psychiatrist

Though she left the funeral and never went back to those people who called themselves a part of the family, but, that was certainly not the end of her struggles. Maybe she left that house that day but every day she was struggling to live. There was no one who can understand her pain as if she became a robot. She goes to the office, as usual, come home and it was just that. She was around people but that was just a noise. She choose not to talk to anyone but that even does not help.

Kanak knew that she cannot spend her entire life in this struggle as it was killing her from inside and thus she took a new way. She checked online and found a Psychiatrist. She was not mad but she needed help. She wants to cry without people judging her. She went to see Dr. Vinay in the morning and sat in the chair. Vinay very calmly looked at her and asked - How do you feel? What is there in your mind? Just be honest, I am not here to judge you. I am here to help you.

Kanak tried being strong at first, telling her about the family, her life, and the death of her mother and sister but as she progresses her story, her eyes suddenly became watery. Kanak said - "*I am not upset over the demise as if I knew it was to happen but was just getting delayed over the years. She [mother] was not happy, I have never seen that woman actually happy in my entire life. She was a giver. Her main goal was to make him [father] happy no matter what. She expected a lot from her [Tamanna] but her expectations broke at every point. I do not blame my sister like everybody else because I have seen the environment she grew up. What makes me actually sad is the people. Everyone, around who thinks of themselves as elders or intelligent or well to do or anything was never there to support her [mother], she asked for help but it was never given to her. It makes me cry to see these people shedding their fake tears when they did not do anything when they have the opportunity. Now they blame my sister, my father, or me [sometimes] but how that is fair. I also do sometimes blame myself, what if that fateful day I was at home. It might be possible that she would not take that harsh step if I was there. She used to love me very much.*

Sometimes, I suddenly wake up from my sleep feeling so suffocated, and sometimes I feel miserable about everything around me, sometimes I just want to cry, and sometimes I just feel awfully lonely even with a bunch of people. I try to be positive but sometimes it's just not there.

I don't feel she has gone, I used to live away from home before so I just feel that she is there, she is at home, everything is just like before. It is just that since I am away and busy with my work, I cannot go home. I always remember her good things like food etc. I do remember my father as well, with his good memories that he is playing with us, etc. As if everything that happened just got vanished. As if it never happened, as if everything is good and is there but it's just that I cannot go home as I am busy."

She didn't realize by while talking to the doctor she was just looking at the tree nearby and tears were falling from the side of her eye and she continues, "*My mother always calls me in the afternoon and wakes me up for the office. That day I did not get her call. To this day, I hope that the phone rang and it's her, but, that never happen. After a few months, I gave up on it. To this day, I never bother to check my phone until I need it urgently. I not only gave up on the people around me but I just gave up on things as well.*" and she sees the doctor. There was a pin drop silence and after a short pause, she again looked at that tree and continues, "*I remember my relatives saying things about my mother and sister that day, I saw them blaming my father as well. But none of them was brave enough to take the ownership. Her [mother] brothers, sisters, and their children and every relative were present in that room, everyone knows what her relationship with her husband is, and how is she had been treated but none of them ever took a stand for her. None of them ever supported her. She needed them. But for them, it was a normal household thing because, in the end, everyone thinks this is normal. Women can be treated in any way. This is the mentality and the sad reality of our nation.*" And then again there was a pause, Kanak wiped her tears and looked at the doctor, and said, "*I tried helping her, I asked her to leave everything, Bikram and Tamanna, and come live with me. I will take care of you always. You deserve to be happy but she [Parvati] said, I can't. This will dishonor my family. I came into this house as a bride and the day I leave this house will be the day I am dead and not before. I was unable to convince her and*

I left. I am not hurt that she died, I feel bad for her choices. I feel hurt that she had the courage to die but not live a life she deserves on her own terms."

Still seeing in the doctor's eyes, Kanak stopped talking, and there was deep silence for a few minutes while Dr. Vinay was analyzing her thoughts and feelings. He was numb and did not have any words to console her because she was not sad. She knew right and wrong. She was not a mess but all she wanted was to be heard. She just wanted someone to listen to the noise in her.

After a while, Dr. Vinay patiently said - "*You need to let it go and I shall give you a few medications*". Kanak was not sure that the medications will help and she never took them. But expressing her feelings definitely did help her as if she has relieved herself from a burden.

XIV

The Void

Years passed and people forget Parvati, Tamanna, Bikram, and Kanak. Everyone was busy and occupied in their own lives and yes that is how life works. There were many unanswered questions, there was guilt, and there was noise but still, there was a void.

There is not always a happy ending for everyone. Years passed and Bikram is having his new family, and I truly pray he should not be behaving and treating her woman like he treated Parvati. Everyone deserves to be happy and loved and so does Bikram. It could be possible that he was not right for Parvati and the family he built was out of family pressure. That may not be quite an explanation for the mistreating he did but as a human, he too deserves a life he thought. If it's not with Parvati then it is fine but he too deserves to be actually happy. Bikram might not be an ideal husband but he was definitely a caring father. And they say sometimes if you care a lot, it only gives you more pain. I wish wherever he would be today, with whom he is, and whatever he learned from his life with Parvati and kids, only would have made him a better person who knows the value of actual love and is happy and growing every day.

Kanak, on other hand, also misses her mother and sister but is well occupied with her career so does not have enough time to just cry on the things that are not there but rather focuses on her own growth as a human. Sometimes, that void hits but that is just a part of life and it's okay to feel sad and down. What is more important is to stand up and walk again with that smile. Her mother always used to tell her, "***people see you sad, they think you are weak and the world always takes advantage of weak people. But you are not a weak person. You are strong, the strongest person I know. You have the courage to take this world down to your feet. You do not need anyone to help you and never ask anything from anyone, not from your family, not from your friends, not from your partner, anyone. Once you ask, you are always in debt to that person, so be independent and show the world that you are anytime better than them and don't care what anyone thinks of you because whatever you will do, you cannot make everyone happy, people will always find a way to make you feel less of yourself. So the plan should be to make yourself happy and do anything which is morally and ethically correct***". And she is doing the same. She does not hate her father or her relatives, it's just that these people do not exist for her anymore. Kanak wakes up every morning but there is something that is always missing. Something she cannot explain and something no one can understand. She might be able to erase the things from her mind so that they shall not bother her anymore but something did die in her as well and she was not the same.

The relatives and neighbors, it's a hi-tea gossip for them. It's not their fault I say, some people take ownership and some don't have the courage to do the same. Also, when I thought about it, it's fine because we live in a society wherein we are driven by society. We do everything to be accepted by them. Today we people have forgotten our identities, and do not want to show what we want and what we are, we just became a herd of sheep who do not have any direction but are just moving. But the sad part is, everyone knows what they did and after a long day of showing off that mask of illusion to everyone, when a person is alone, the wrongs haunt them. Becoming a true version of oneself is not easy and acceptable but it is necessary in order to not live a life without regrets and guilt and just to move on.

But in the end, what is always there is a void. Over a period of time, all the bad memories fade, and then all the good ones too, and what remains is emptiness.

XV

Who Was The Culprit?

I wrote the whole story but I really do not have an ending for this because I don't understand who is the actual culprit - Parvati, Bikram, Tamanna, Kanak, Parvati's choices, the society they live in, Parvati's family, the situation or I am not sure if I am missing something.................!!!

End Credits

"*With the success of my first Book -* **"Unapologetic Words"**, *I am glad to introduce my second book -* **"Unapologetic Scribbles - A Journey Of Broken Expectations"** *which is more of a story-telling.*

Follow me on Instagram - **@memoni_ka**

Check out my blogs @
geminimonika92.wordpress.com
geminimonika92.blogspot.com"

9 798887 172187

Printed by Libri Plureos GmbH in Hamburg, Germany